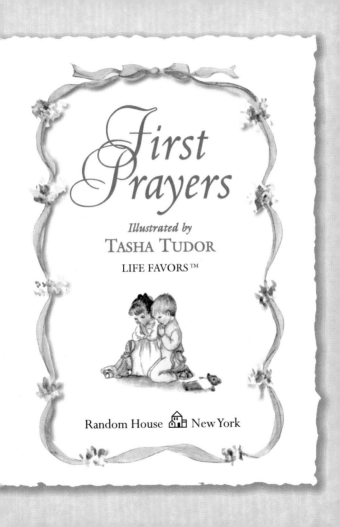

First Prayers

Illustrated by
TASHA TUDOR

LIFE FAVORS™

Random House New York

The Lord bless us, and keep us.
The Lord make his face to shine upon
   us, and be gracious unto us.
The Lord lift up his countenance upon us,
   and give us peace, both now and
   evermore.

                    Amen.

The Lord's Prayer

Our Father which art in heaven,
Hallowed be thy name.
Thy Kingdom come.
Thy will be done
in earth as it is in heaven.
Give us this day our daily bread.
And forgive us our debts,
as we forgive our debtors.
And lead us not into temptation,
but deliver us from evil:
For Thine is the kingdom,
and the power, and the glory,
For ever. Amen.

IN THE MORNING

Father in Heaven, all through the night
I have been sleeping, safe in Thy sight.
Father, I thank Thee; bless me, I pray,
Bless me and keep me all through the
    day.

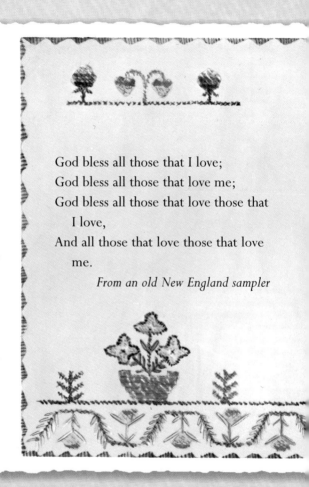

God bless all those that I love;
God bless all those that love me;
God bless all those that love those that
  I love,
And all those that love those that love
  me.

From an old New England sampler

O Holy Jesus,
Most merciful Redeemer,
Friend and brother,
May I know Thee more clearly,
Love Thee more dearly,
And follow Thee more nearly.

Amen.

St. Richard of Chichester

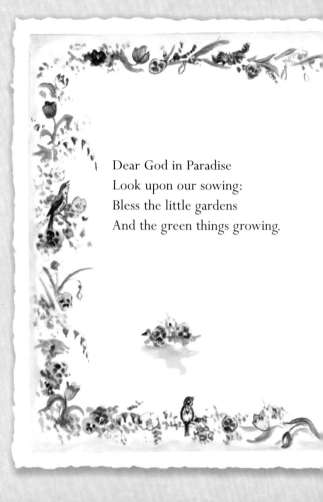

Dear God in Paradise
Look upon our sowing:
Bless the little gardens
And the green things growing.

GRACE BEFORE AND AFTER MEAT

Bless me, O Lord, and let my food
strengthen me to serve Thee,
for Jesus Christ's sake. Amen.

The New England Primer

Thou art great
And Thou art good,
And we thank Thee
For this food.
By Thy hand
Must all be fed,
And we thank Thee
For this bread.

GENTLE JESUS, MEEK AND MILD

Gentle Jesus, meek and mild,
Look upon a little child;
Pity my simplicity,
Suffer me to come to Thee.

Fain I would to Thee be brought;
Dearest God, forbid it not:
Give me, dearest God, a place
In the kingdom of Thy grace.

Put Thy hands upon my head,
Let me in Thine arms be stayed;
Let me lean upon Thy breast,
Lull me, lull me, Lord, to rest.

Hold me fast in Thy embrace,
Let me see Thy smiling face.
Give me, Lord, Thy blessing give;
Pray for me, and I shall live.

Lamb of God, I look to Thee;
Thou shalt my Example be;
Thou are gentle, meek and mild,
Thou wast once a little Child.

Fain I would be as Thou art;
Give me Thy obedient heart.
Thou art pitiful and kind;
Let me have Thy loving mind.

NOW THE DAY IS OVER

Now the day is over,
Night is drawing nigh,
Shadows of the evening
Steal across the sky;

Jesus, give the weary
Calm and sweet repose;
With thy tenderest blessing
May our eyelids close.

Grant to little children
Visions bright of thee;
Guard the sailors tossing
On the deep blue sea.

Comfort every sufferer
Watching late in pain;
Those who plan some evil
From their sins restrain.

Through the long night watches,
May thine angels spread
Their white wings above me,
Watching round my bed.

When the morning wakens,
Then may I arise
Pure and fresh and sinless
In thy holy eyes.

Sabine Baring-Gould

THE TWENTY-THIRD PSALM

The Lord is my shepherd; I shall not
   want.
He maketh me to lie down in green
   pastures:
He leadeth me beside the still waters.
He restoreth my soul: he leadeth me
   in the paths of righteousness for
   his name's sake.

Yea, though I walk through the valley of
the shadow of death, I will fear no
evil:
For thou art with me; thy rod and thy
staff they comfort me.
Thou preparest a table before me in the
presence of mine enemies:
Thou anointest my head with oil;
My cup runneth over.
Surely goodness and mercy shall follow
me all the days of my life:
And I will dwell in the house of the Lord
for ever.

CRADLE HYMN

Away in a manger, no crib for a bed,
The little Lord Jesus laid down his sweet
  head.
The stars in the bright sky looked down
  where he lay—
The little Lord Jesus asleep on the hay.

The cattle are lowing, the baby awakes,
But little Lord Jesus no crying he makes.
I love Thee, Lord Jesus! Look down
    from the sky,
And stay by my cradle till morning is
    nigh.

Be near me, Lord Jesus, I ask Thee to
    stay
Close by me forever, and love me, I
    pray.
Bless all the dear children, in Thy
    tender care,
And take us to heaven, to live with
    Thee there.

Martin Luther